PERSONAL PROBLEMS

Four short stories from the
Postcards from Earth Collection.

Tom Sterling

Copyright

Personal Problems
© 2024 by Tom Sterling

www.tomsterling.com

This book is a work of fiction. Names, characters, places, and incidents are either the product of the author's imagination or are used fictitiously. Any resemblance to actual events, locales, or persons, living or dead, is entirely coincidental.

ALL RIGHTS RESERVED. No part of this work may be reproduced or transmitted in any form or by any means without the author's written permission unless such copying is expressly permitted by federal and international copyright laws, or for the purpose of small excerpts embodied in critical articles and reviews.

Inquiries concerning reproduction or publication outside the scope of the above should be directed to the author via the contact form on the web address above.

ISBN: 978-1-958864-39-5

Edited by Christine Cartwright

Cover design by Sam Sterling

SAMUEL STERLING
3D MODELER & TEXTURE ARTIST
Website ArtStation Linkedin

Picture on Page 27:
My Dream, My Bad Dream – Fritz Schwimbeck (upper corner)
https://upload.wikimedia.org/wikipedia/commons/0/05/Fritz_Schwimbeck_-_My_Dream%2C_My_Bad_Dream._1915.jpg
This work is in the public domain

Dedication

To the little room with the lock on the outside in the attic of our old house. Where I first learned that monsters are real.

About this Book

These four stories began as a stretch goal for myself. I wanted to see if I could write a short story fit for a *Noir at the Bar* event, read my story in front of an audience, and entertain them. Could I make them laugh, smile, or just be surprised?

Reading **_Nothing Personal_** at the event was a wonderful experience for me. Writers in the audience were encouraging and gracious, and seemed to enjoy my story about a human boy meeting a vampire girl in a bar.

Afterward, I realized Bill's tale wasn't finished and wrote three more chapters to reveal a little more of the story.

Table of Contents

Copyright iv
Dedication vii
About this Book ix
Table of Contents xi
PFE #13—Nothing Personal 13
PFE #17—Now It Is Personal 21
PFE #19—A Personal Favor 29
PFE #20—My Personal Space 43
Acknowledgements 73
About the Author 75

Postcards from Earth

PFE #13—Nothing Personal

Nothing Personal

Bill just turned twenty-one. He's been waiting for this day his entire life, and planning what he would do when the day finally arrived.

Mom always warned him that nothing good happens after midnight. Tonight, Bill is going to find out if Mom was right.

Postcards from Earth

Nothing Personal

(Bill's Tale)

"I used to come here in my twenties," says the beautiful woman sitting next to me at the bar. "Back then, it was called The Library, and when my mom and dad asked where I was going at night, I'd just say I was going to the library."

She chuckles. "And they never caught on, even with that big Library Disco sign sitting right out on Main Street."

"I thought you were in your twenties," I say. "You seem like just another university student out on a Thursday night."

She smiles and runs fingers through glossy, raven-black hair. "That's nice of you to say, but you and I aren't even in the same decade. Back when I used to come here, there was a disco ball and colored lights built right into the dance floor, just like that movie, *Saturday Night Fever*. My friends and I used to meet here every week and get down to music from Billy Idol and Flock of Seagulls. I'm probably old enough to be your—mom's older sister."

She adjusts on the barstool revealing a very narrow waist and long, shapely brown legs. Her movements are like a dancer's, and the scent of flowers floats in the air as she turns.

"I'm Ani," she says.

"I'm Bill," I answer. "And today's my twenty-first birthday. You feel like having a drink with me to celebrate?"

Nothing Personal

Her cheeks flush, and when her soft, mahogany-brown eyes look into mine, it feels like they gaze directly into my soul. "You know, Bill, I would love that."

Her lithe body flows like bamboo in the wind as she leans back and glances down the bar. "No friends here to help you celebrate?"

"Just me tonight," I say. "I thought about asking a few friends, but this birthday feels kind of personal to me. You know what I mean?"

I wave the bartender over and order an Old Fashioned, which used to be my father's favorite drink.

"And whatever my friend Ani here is having," I add.

"I think I'd like a Sloe Comfortable Screw," she says to the bartender, who nods and steps away to make the drinks.

She blushes again and focuses back on my eyes. Shiny specks sparkle and swirl within the deep brown of her irises.

"I always feel self-conscious ordering that drink, but it used to be the bar's specialty back in the day, and it's good."

She smiles and reaches over, lightly stroking the back of my hand. Currents of electricity seem to jump off her fingers to every corner of my body.

"Did you just ask me to be your first?" she teases. "That feels kind of personal, too." She never takes her eyes off mine, and I feel my body pulling toward her—like I'm falling.

"Did you mean first drinking buddy—or something else?" she adds, giggling, and removing her hand as if noticing her touch's effect on me. Our conversation must feel like some kind of game to her. One she isn't sure she wants to play.

The bartender reappears with our drinks, breaking up the awkward moment.

I lift my glass in a toast. "First anything you want it to be, Ani."

If this woman wants to play, then I'm all in.

I inhale the fresh orange and cherry aroma of my Old Fashioned and take my first sip. Not as good as a Coke, but I like it. My throat heats up when I swallow it down.

Ani takes a long, slow drink of her cocktail. She closes her eyes as if savoring the sweet taste. Maybe it brings back memories of those hot nights years ago on the disco floor.

"You never forget your first, that's for sure," she says after a time. "My first was with Victor—right here in this very bar. He was a bit older, but he looked kind of like you. He was tall, dark, sophisticated—and that man could dance!"

She flashes a smile, and her cheeks redden.

"He could—" She stops mid-sentence as if trying to remember something important. Seconds tick by. She furrows her brows. "Victor could—" More seconds tick by. Finally, she lets out a soft sigh and turns back toward me.

This time, her eyes stare into mine with raw hunger. The swirling flecks in her irises pull me in like a magnet toward steel. Before I know what is happening, we're locked in a heated kiss, and my hand is gripping her warm, smooth leg. Blood pounds in my eardrums, and I fight just to maintain control.

I start fumbling with Ani's clothing right there at the bar. I can't help myself.

She pushes me away and stands up. Her face is hard like stone.

Game over, I think.

"Finish your drink and pay," she commands. She turns toward the door.

I gulp down my drink and throw down some cash. My whole body feels out of balance.

"Follow me," she instructs as she leaves.

I stumble behind her like a lost puppy. All my eyes can see is the subtle sway of her hips.

She leads me down an alley and stops in front of a faded, red Ford Mustang.

"Get in," she says, holding open the passenger door.

I flop down on the black vinyl seat. Every nerve is on fire.

Ani climbs in onto my lap, facing me. Her body soft and warm. Her perfume intoxicating. She shuts the car door, and the dome light goes out. Her body shimmers faintly in the darkness. She leans forward, and her long hair falls all around my face. Every strand flows with electricity.

Ani's dark, sparkly eyes look deep into mine, and as I watch, her pupils begin to glow with a red inner fire. She strokes my cheek and pulls my shirt collar away from my neck.

"Happy Birthday, Bill," she says, baring long, razor-sharp cuspids.

"I want you to know that this really is nothing—personal . . . ."

"Victor was my father," I say, jamming my Sig Sauer P239 into the base of her neck. I pull the trigger eight times until the pistol stops firing.

"It's personal to me."

Nothing Personal

PFE #17—Now It Is Personal

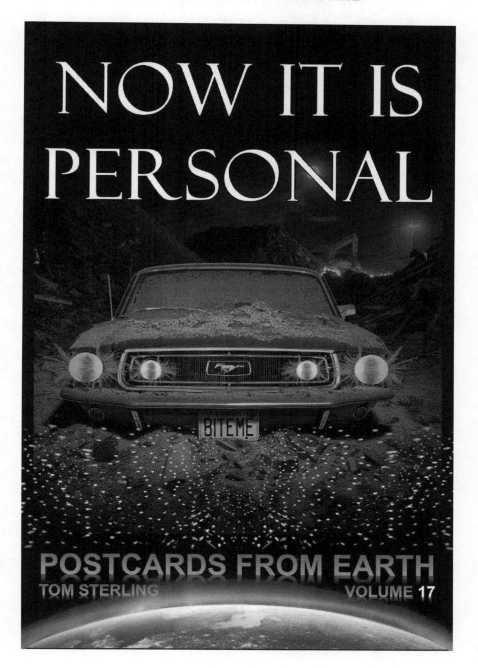

Now It Is Personal

Ani was just shot in the head multiple times and left for dead. Her broken body was tossed into the trunk of a car and buried in a landfill burn pit.

It wasn't her worst Thursday night.

Postcards from Earth

Now It Is Personal

(Ani's Tale)

I wake up in the trunk of my car. I know it's my car because I recognize the Mindblower speakers I installed back in the '70s, and my backpack sits right where I tossed it before tonight's hunt. The bones in my neck are slowly knitting themselves back together, but it'll be a minute or two before I can move anything other than my eyes.

Birthday Boy didn't kill me.

He sure as hell got the drop on me, though. I've got to give the man that. But like so many other stupid college boys I've known, once Bill shot off his gun, he left without finishing the job. And as soon as I'm strong enough to move, Bill is going to pay for that mistake.

Now, it *is* personal.

And to think that, back in the bar, I was actually starting to like Bill. He wasn't going to be just another frat boy snack. I was thinking about putting him on a regular meal plan.

My body lies in a twisted heap across the floor of the trunk. When my eyes adjust to the darkness, I see how much blood soaked into my brand-new Zara dress. Bill's going to pay for that, too. I just bought this dress.

Next comes the part of the healing I dread. Explosions of pain rock my body as nerves weave back together one by one. Cramped muscles cry out in agony. Scrapes and bruises scream from where Bill dragged me across the sharp steel edges of the trunk opening. That man is *so* going to regret this night by the time I'm through with him.

My pain subsides to dull burning, and when I'm able to move, I roll toward the taillights, pull a knife out of my backpack, and pry at the trunk latch until the lid pops open.

"Ready or not, Bill. Here I come!" I mutter, scrambling out of the trunk. I flop over onto the ground, and my bare feet sink into a thick pile of soot and ash. My car is buried up to the bumpers in the stuff. It looks like College Boy tried to burn me and my Mustang in the landfill burn pit and failed at that, too.

I pull fresh clothes from my backpack and do a quick change right there in the burn pit. If someone gets a free peepshow, oh well. They'd just better not let me catch them, though, because I'm hungry. I dig my phone, keys, and a bag of Reese's Pieces out of the backpack and munch on the candy while checking the time. Still a few hours until sunrise. I should go home and regroup, but I really want to see the look on Birthday Boy's face when I show up at his house tonight.

I shift the Mustang into neutral, grab the front bumper, and shove my car out of the burn pit until all four wheels are on solid ground. Gray ash gets on everything, including the brand-new Adidas tennis shoes I just pulled on. Bill's tab keeps growing, and I begin thinking up creative things to do to him. But first, I've got to find him.

Bill provided a clue right before shooting me when he said that Victor was his father. I know exactly where Victor used to live. Years ago, Victor was my dance partner, playmate, and regular Thursday night meal before he passed away at the ripe old age of twenty-four. I even loved Victor, in my way, and I felt sad when his connection to me snapped.

I drive to the north side of town and park in my old spot near Victor's house. A well-worn path leads through the shadows of some trees to an old colonial home. I smell Birthday Boy inside, along with someone I haven't smelled in years: Victor's wife, Rachel.

I leap up and grab the branch of an oak tree overhanging the porch, dangle my legs until my feet touch shingles, and drop silently onto the roof. The intoxicating Bill aroma is coming from a window on the left, where the sash is pulled up a few inches. Inside, I see Birthday Boy sleeping like a log, exhausted from his long night of killing me.

I use my fingernail to slice an opening in the screen large enough to climb through. Victor used to beg me to visit him here, and I feel no compulsion against raising the window and easing myself into the room. Just like old times.

Breathing in Bill's delicious aroma, I think about how much he looks like his father, and my rage transforms into a misty combination of loss, hunger, and lust. I decide to play with Bill for a while before killing him.

I jam my fingernail into my wrist until a few drops of dark blood seep out. Slurping the blood into my mouth, I lean over Bill's face and touch my lips against his. Bill responds as only a twenty-one-year-old man can, and for a glorious few minutes, we're young lovers making out on the bed while Mom is sleeping in the next room.

Now It Is Personal

I feel the bond begin to form in Bill's mind as the blood he ingests does its thing, and when my new servant's ice-blue eyes blink open, they gaze into mine with love and devotion. His body responds with rapture at my touch.

Birthday Boy is mine.

There are just two more things to do before letting my new plaything get some rest. First of all, I'm starving! I extract my fangs and bite down hard on Bill's neck just above his collarbone. Bill gasps in pain, but the pain turns to ecstasy as hormones in my saliva send waves of pleasure surging through his body. Bill's blood is exquisite, like a top cut of steak, and I feel his strength flowing into me as I drink.

I execute the final test of our bond and show him my true form, unfolding long, leathery wings and revealing gray, unliving flesh. The devotion in Bill's eyes never wavers, and he pulls me down into a passionate kiss.

There's an explosion of pain as something slams into my neck. My body slumps forward, and I see Victor's wife, Rachel, standing over me with a lumber maul. My blood spurts out onto the bedsheets.

"Nooo!" moans Bill as his mother steps up to take another swing. "Don't hurt her, Mom! I love her!"

"Get away from that thing, Billy," hisses Rachel. "It's not human!"

Rachel swings the axe again, shattering several bones in my spine. Another blast of pain and then—nothing. For the second time tonight, I can't feel my body. I gasp, "Stop her!" but before Bill can move, Rachel throws down the axe and pulls out a pistol. "I said get away from it!"

Bill crawls off the bed and slinks into a corner of the room. So much for our special bond. Bill turns out to be just another Momma's Boy.

I stare defiantly into the woman's hate-filled eyes. Blood gurgles from my neck as I wheeze out, "You can't kill me, Rachel. I'll be back . . ."

"I remember you, Ani," says Rachel. "And I know what you are. I'm not afraid of you."

She leans over until her mouth is right next to my ear.

"Just who do you think killed Victor?"

Now It Is Personal

Postcards from Earth

PFE #19—A Personal Favor

My Personal Space

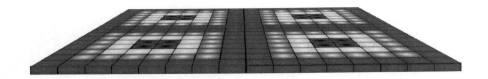

Left no good deed unpunished, no bad one unrewarded.

- Knight Eudo from Walter Map's De Nugis Curialium

In this prequel to **Nothing Personal** and **Now It Is Personal**, we follow along with Victor as he decides to do a favor for his best friend, Barry.

A small white lie leads Victor out onto the colorful disco floor and into a dark world he never knew existed.

Postcards from Earth

A Personal Favor

(Victor's Tale – 20 years earlier)

I'm just about to drop another quarter into the Galaxian machine when my pager goes off. At first, I ignore the beeps, thinking they're part of the game. Then I feel an urgent vibration on my hip, glance down, and see the phone number. My buddy Barry is checking in.

Whipping my Nokia out of its belt holster, I press speed dial number two. When Barry picks up, I growl, "Wazzzuuuupp?" loud and low into the mouthpiece. An elderly couple in the booth next to the game room turn and shake their heads at me. The lady looks incensed, but the old man is stifling a laugh.

Barry echoes "Wazzzuuuupp?" back at me and gets to the point of his call. "What are you doing tonight, V?" he asks. "The Library just remodeled their dance floor, and it looks exactly like that *Saturday Night Fever* movie. Time to go bust a move!"

A night on the town with Barry sounds perfect right now. I've been staring at boring Government software code for months, mitigating Y2K problems, and frankly, I need a break. And hanging out with Barry is always a blast. He's one of those odd force of nature types that attracts both magic and mayhem to him wherever he goes. A night out with Barry always feels like it could end up with the two of us sitting on a yacht someplace in the middle of the Caribbean, or possibly behind bars.

"That sounds cool, brother, but I can't tonight," I say. "I'm at Tony's picking up a pizza. I TiVo'ed *The Sopranos*, and Rachel and I are going to watch it together as soon as Billy's in bed. Between Y2K and that little rugrat coming along, we haven't had much 'us' time, if you know what I mean."

"C'mon, man!" pleads Barry. "It's got to be tonight. That chick Kate I told you about was spotted at the club last night, and I need you there as my wingman. She was with her assistant, Ani, and those two always show up both Wednesday and Thursday nights when they're in town. I already tipped DJ Rob to play "Kiss Me" by that group Sixpence None the Richer if he sees me dancing with her. I heard it's her favorite song."

"I don't know, dude," I say. "I'm already in deep kimchee for working both days last weekend. Rachel needs a break, and I sure as hell don't want her calling up the outlaws for help. Her mom stayed for two months the last time she was here."

"C'mon, V. I need this!" begs Barry again. "I'll owe you one, big time. Help a brother out!"

The phone goes silent, and I can picture the wheels in Barry's head start turning as he tries to figure out what he can say to change my mind. I already know it's impossible.

"I'll babysit for you all day long on Saturday."

I stand corrected. The impossible just became possible. Magic Barry does it again. But telling Rachel I'm going out drinking and dancing on a Thursday night after abandoning her all weekend is still a non-starter. I need to come up with a good lie—for both of our sakes.

The wheels in my own head start turning.

Postcards from Earth

* * *

I come up with a plan, and if I say so myself, it's pure genius. After bringing home the pizza, I spring my deception on Rachel between bites of Tony's delicious Sicilian Special. The conversation goes exactly like it did in my head, and technically, I never lie to her.

"What do you mean you have to go back out?" says Rachel. "I thought tonight was *Sopranos* night."

"I'm sorry, honey, but I have to go to the library." *The Library Disco, that is.*

"Another late night?" she asks. "I thought last weekend was the end of the overtime for a while."

"I have one last thing to work on." *Barry's love life.*

"Well, we can use the money, I guess. How late will you be?"

"There's no way of knowing for sure. I could end up turning right around and coming back home. It depends on who shows up and how much we get done." *I'm only planning to be there long enough for Barry to ask Kate to dance. If she doesn't show up or turns him down, I'll be home before the pizza cools off.*

"Oh, and guess what? Barry volunteered to babysit Billy for us on Saturday. We can go out on a real date. Just you and me!"

Pure genius.

* * *

My Personal Space

TLC's "No Scrubs" is playing as we walk up to the nightclub. DJ Rob always starts his Thursday night gigs with a set he calls "Girl Power" to lure college ladies into the club. The songs must be working tonight because the line goes up the stairs and halfway down the block. Barry's a regular here, and when Wally, the doorman, spots us, he calls us up to the front of the line and waves us on through. I grab a table by the dance floor while Barry squeezes in at the bar to check in with Jimmy the bartender and start a tab. The tempo picks up, and the deep base of "Groove is in the Heart" by Deee-Lite starts playing just as Barry shows up with my Old Fashioned and a Gin and Juice for himself.

"I think it's finally going down tonight, brother," he says with a hopeful look on his face. "Kate and Ani are in one of the back booths. They're arguing about something, but at least there aren't any swinging Richards loitering around."

"So, you're telling me there's a chance," I say, smiling back and doing my best *Dumb and Dumber* impersonation over the throbbing beat of the music. We clink glasses, fire up a couple of Marlboros, and watch through clouds of smoke as the multicolored squares on the new dance floor light up in time to the music. I make a note to ask DJ Rob if he programmed all those colorful patterns himself or if the floor came that way. The lights do look like *Saturday Night Fever*, though, so props either way.

As if to emphasize the point, "You Should Be Dancing" by the Bee Gees starts blasting out of the JBL tower speakers. Before we know what hits us, a gaggle of college babes in miniskirts swoops down on our table and tries to drag us onto the dance floor. That's life with Magic Barry! I resist and tell my girl, Cindy, that I'm married, but I don't think she hears me, and moments later, we're all out doing the hustle. I lie and tell myself I'm doing it for my upcoming date night with Rachel, but the truth is, I'm enjoying the chance to blow off some steam.

The music transitions down to the first slow song of the night, another Bee Gees hit called "How Deep is Your Love." I pull away from Cindy and head back toward the table when a burst of red catches my eye. That girl Barry wants to meet, Kate, is making her entrance onto the dance floor, wearing a silky, form-fitting slip dress the color of red wine. Lustrous, ebony hair drapes like satin all the way down to a tiny waist.

DJ Rob must have seen Kate walking up because a swirling cluster of tiny spotlights starts tracking her every move as she struts over to the DJ booth. Watching the circles of light dance across Kate's lithe body, I see why my buddy is so hung up on her. Barry's a great guy but can be a little shallow in the dating department. It's all about looks and attitude to him. And judging by the other male gazes around the room scoping out Kate, he's not alone. The swirling lights reflecting off Kate's bright red dress begin to remind me of those laser gunsight dots in sniper movies.

Ani steps out under the lights a few paces behind Kate, and in any other universe, she would be the center of attention. If Kate is a ten, Ani is a solid, nine-point-nine. She looks like a young Naomi Campbell, wearing a slip dress like Kate's, only Ani's is the color of crisp white bedsheets. Another difference between the two women is their attitudes.

My Personal Space

Kate looks ready to party, but Ani looks like she wants to fade into the shadowy, smoke-filled corners of the room.

"It's go time!" says Barry, blowing a cone of smoke over his shoulder and taking a big gulp of his drink. "C'mon, V, let's do this thing."

Barry pushes back his chair and makes a beeline for Kate. I follow behind, loitering far enough back so that I can veer off to the bathroom if they start dancing. Barry steps up to the plate and takes his swing like the player he is. It looks like he's about to score a hit when suddenly Ani jumps between the two of them and grabs Kate's hand. I can't understand what they're saying in all the commotion, but I do hear a loud *smack* when Kate slaps Ani across the face. I decide to play umpire and step up in time to see Ani release Kate's hand and start crying. Pulling a handkerchief out of my pocket, I offer it to Ani as Barry, Kate, and the cluster of swirling disco lights shift a few feet away and start dancing.

"I'm Victor," I say as Ani takes the offered handkerchief. "And that's my buddy, Barry." I lift up my hand and point to my wedding ring. "I'd normally be home eating pizza and watching *The Sopranos* right now, but Barry wanted to meet your girl, Kate, and he asked me to come out with him tonight. So here I am, out on the town, as a personal favor to my best friend. You don't have to worry about Barry, though, Ani. I've known him all my life, and he's one of the good ones."

Ani's lip is bleeding, and there's a bright red handprint forming on the left side of her face.

"Can I offer you a drink?" I ask. "Jimmy's working the bar tonight and can make just about anything. Our table is right near the dance floor, so you can keep an eye on Kate if you want."

"Thank you," says Ani, sniffing and dabbing at tears. "A drink would be okay, I guess." She sits down and focuses on Kate while I head to the bar. When I get back to the table, Barry and Kate are dancing to "Linger" by The Cranberries, and Ani can't seem to stop crying. I set a Cosmopolitan down on a napkin in front of her and hope she doesn't notice that the drink is the same color as Kate's dress. I raise my Old Fashioned in a toast.

"When I was a kid, my father always used to say, 'One drink makes you feel good, two drinks make you feel better, and three drinks make you fall asleep so Daddy can watch football.'"

Ani smiles, takes a big slurp of her cocktail, and pulls a slim pack of clove cigarettes out of her purse. I flick my Bic and watch a glimmer of satisfaction on Ani's face as she takes a long drag and blows the spicy smoke straight up into the air.

Then I go and run my big mouth. "What happened out there, Ani?" I ask. "Did Kate fire you or something?"

Ani's face turns hard like stone.

"Something like that," she says. "But it's more like a promotion, really. A promotion I never asked for or wanted. I'm not sure I'm ready."

"Linger" fades away, and Barry's song pick, "Kiss Me," begins flowing out of the speakers. The disco lights dim, and hundreds of tiny, incandescent bulbs twinkle like stars across the ceiling overhead. Kate and Barry cling to one another and float across the dance floor through a sea of other young couples.

"I'm sure you'll do just fine," I say, wanting to comfort her but not having a clue what she's talking about. Tiny flecks of green and gold begin to flicker like fireworks within Ani's deep brown eyes as she stares across the room at her friend.

"Maybe it's time to find out," says Ani, turning to beam those stunning mahogany irises in my direction. "I'm so sorry, Victor," I hear as the flecks of light in her eyes begin to sparkle and swirl, gripping my attention and preventing me from looking away. Her eyes drag me toward her like gravity pulling a plane down out of the sky, and I careen, out of control, directly into her soft lips. Her kiss is warm and wet, with subtle, sweet flavors of anise, honey, and cinnamon—like Greek fennel cookies fresh from the oven washed down with a shot of Ouzo.

But Ani's attractive force doesn't stop there. The noise of the crowded bar diminishes and fades away as Ani pulls me past her lips to a place deep inside of herself. I feel a connection form between us, and suddenly, Ani is inside my head, reading my thoughts like I'm an open encyclopedia. In seconds, I change from being only *me* to becoming part of a *we*, staring at *ourselves* across the table from two separate chairs. Gazing into Ani's eyes, I'm also staring out of those eyes, watching the puzzled look on my face as I try to understand what's happening to me.

The engineering geek in me wonders if this is what computers feel like when they connect over the internet, and I sense Ani's laughter in my head at the thought. My mind races toward that laughter, and I feel Ani's surprise and fear as we discover together that I can also enter *her* mind and search *her* memories. I find out that Ani is actually much older and that she's been Kate's thrall for the past 17 years. Now I understand their strange, symbiotic relationship, and I can feel Ani's lingering agony from Kate severing their own mental connection earlier this evening—and the pain of being tossed aside after all those years of devotion. I see the horror of Kate's true vampire form. I even feel Ani's concern over my friend Barry and her fear of what Kate might do to him.

From the alarms going off in Ani's head, I can tell that our connection isn't working the way she thought it would. I'm her very first victim, and she only intended to play with me for a while, drain me of some of my blood, and leave me sleeping in the alley outside the bar as a distraction to take her mind off of Kate. Instead, her poisonous kiss somehow formed a powerful link between our two minds, affecting her just as much as it did me. As we computer geeks would say, our connection is bi-directional. We're bonded together, both mentally and emotionally.

And looking across the table into Ani's soft brown eyes, I'm okay with that. In those few short moments following our kiss, I've fallen in love with her. My feelings for my wife, Rachel, haven't changed. But this bond with Ani feels more intimate, somehow. Maybe something in Ani's saliva causes this sensation, but the connection feels real. I sense Ani's every thought—her every emotion—and every nerve ending in her body—as if they're my own. Ani is a part of me now—and it's intoxicating.

My Personal Space

Moments earlier, I didn't even believe that vampires existed. Now, I would do anything to maintain this connection with Ani. Anything.

And I sense that Ani feels the same way about me. She pulls at my mind again, and our bond grows even more intimate. Throwing back our chairs, we wind our way across the crowded dance floor. We race down a dingy, smoke-filled hallway, burst through the back door, and run out into the alley, holding hands under the starry night sky.

I've never felt so connected to my surroundings or seen with such clarity. I look up at the Milky Way and can pick out individual stars. We gaze together as a meteor streaks across the sky between the graffiti-covered brick walls of the alleyway. We marvel at glowing fireflies dancing among the weeds as we make our way to my car. The last things I remember before drifting away in a cloud of ecstasy are hearing the car door shutting softly behind me and the coppery taste of blood in my mouth.

* * *

I wake up in my own bed, feeling refreshed, with my wife, Rachel, sleeping quietly beside me. For the first time since Billy was born, I finally got enough rest.

I'm not completely sure if last night was real or just a dream, but all I can think about are the flecks of light swirling around Ani's brown eyes and that strange, incredible kiss. I go to the bathroom, lock the door behind me, and look at myself in the mirror. I'm a little pale, but otherwise, look the same as always. The only thing out of place is a fading rash above my collarbone.

I return to the bedroom, kiss Rachel on the forehead, check in on Billy, and make my way down to the kitchen for a cup of strong coffee. If the lies, dancing, and kissing really happened, then my actions last night were unforgivable. I'm a married man with a young child, for God's sake, and I truly love my wife. I can't be running around in back alleys kissing strange women.

But as I'm sipping my coffee, I feel a familiar sensation as the connection in my mind begins forming. Ani is calling out to me from a hotel room across town. I resist her summons at first, thinking about my wife and child slumbering peacefully in their beds.

Then I grab my wallet and car keys off of the counter and slip quietly out the door.

My Personal Space

Postcards from Earth

PFE #20—My Personal Space

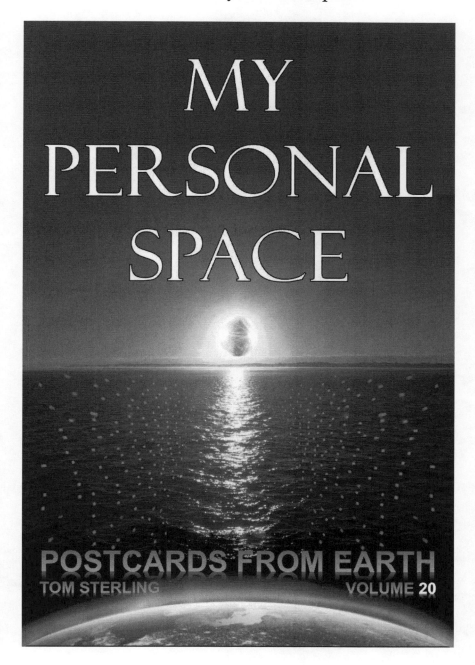

My Personal Space

If you write a problem down clearly, then the problem is half solved.

- Kidlin's Law of Problem Solving

In this sequel to **A Personal Favor**, Rachel tries to determine if her husband Victor might possibly be a vampire.

And whether or not she needs to kill him.

Postcards from Earth

My Personal Space

(Rachel's Tale – still 20 years earlier)

<u>Monday</u>

Something's going on with my husband.

I can't quite put my finger on it, exactly, but Victor is acting differently.

I guess, technically, he's acting better. New Victor is more thoughtful and caring. He does more around the house and pays more attention to me. New Victor also seems to cherish his time with our son Billy and spends hours reading books and playing baby games. When New Victor is with us, he's right there with us the entire time, as if he's savoring every moment.

It's bugging the hell out of me.

Not because he's acting better. I love that. And not because Old Victor wasn't already a good husband. He was. From the moment Victor said "I do" to me, he did. I always felt loved, honored, and cherished. Maybe that's the reason this change is so noticeable. Old Victor was already great. New Victor doesn't feel real.

The change started several months ago when Victor's best friend Barry disappeared. For as long as I've known Victor, those two were inseparable. Then Barry dropped off the map one day and didn't respond to any of Victor's pages or calls. We joked about it at first, thinking Magic Barry was pulling one of his famous disappearing acts. A few days earlier, he had promised to babysit little Billy, and we assumed ghosting us was his way of backing out. Then Barry's BMW was spotted in a ravine outside Wardensville, West Virginia, and things got real.

Victor took time off from work and spent the next four weeks combing the hillsides between Baker and Capon Lake for any signs of his friend. He contacted local police and hospitals in the area. Victor even called Barry's coworkers and relatives. He never found a single clue, and Old Victor never came home. Instead, we got New Victor, and something is definitely wrong with him.

* * *

"What time did you come to bed last night?" I ask, filling our mugs up to the brim with steaming hot coffee.

Victor lifts his cup to his nose, breathing in the rich aroma, while I use a fork to pull two buttery croissants out of the oven. Sitting down at the table for breakfast is our thing, and I cherish every second of this peaceful, thirty-minute window we allot ourselves each day before heading off to work. Some days, we watch the news or read the paper. Other days, we talk or sit in silence, enjoying each other's company. Today, we're listening to a new CD by that Irish band, The Cranberries. I'm paranoid for thinking it, but this feels like another New Victor thing. Old Victor loved music, but I don't remember him ever buying a single CD. And when the first song on the album begins playing, I catch him staring wistfully off into the distance.

"Around 11:30," he says, giving me his best New Victor smile. "You were out of it, and Billy was doing that grunting thing he does when he's about to pop awake." Victor winked. "I told him the mommy bar was closed, gave him a bottle, and rocked him on the front porch until he fell back to sleep."

New Victor looks five years younger than Old Victor, I think, smiling and nodding.

"Well, thanks for that, but don't forget you need your rest, too," I mumble as Victor wolfs down half of his croissant in two quick bites. "Remember, I agreed to handle the night shift when we decided I should stay home for Billy's first year." *And ten years younger than I feel,* I add, grateful for the extra hours of sleep.

Victor stands and stretches. "Speaking of shiftwork, I'd better get going," he says. "That Epochalypse Superbug isn't going to fix itself."

Before I can remind Victor that he has years to solve the Y2K38 problem, he kisses me on the forehead, grabs his keys off the table, and disappears through the garage door. The steady drumbeat of "Dreams" begins thumping out of the CD player, mixing with the deep rumble of the garage door rolling slowly open. I watch my husband's car back out of the driveway as Cranberries lead singer Dolores O'Riordan sings about how her life is changing every day in every possible way.

"Tell me about it, Dolores," I mutter, glancing at the clock and noting that the time is now 7:40. New Victor just cut our half hour of "us" time down to ten minutes.

I turn and spot Victor's lunch bag sitting on the counter in its usual place. That, at least, feels more like Old Victor, who was always a bit absentminded. I stick the bag in the refrigerator and make plans to drop it off at lunchtime. I work at the same small engineering firm as Victor but took off for a year to stay home with little Billy. My badge still works in all the doors, and it'll be nice to walk around and say hi to a few friends.

I hear Billy moving around in his crib just as Dolores begins her long yodeling runs at the end of "Dreams." Taking a last bite of my croissant, I head upstairs.

* * *

At 11:00, I lift Billy into his carrier and lock it in place in the back seat of my Jeep Cherokee. After loading another fifty-odd pounds of baby gear in the back, I slide in behind the wheel. We leave that sad bologna and cheese sandwich Victor made sitting in the refrigerator and stop by the 29 Diner for some real food. Meeting for lunch will be a nice surprise for Victor and a good way for me to get my twenty minutes of "us" time back. I'm surprised when I stop by the reception desk and get the news.

"But he took off a couple of hours ago," says Marta. She shows me a note Victor left with a phone number and address in case someone needs to get in contact with him. "He said he's helping a friend move."

* * *

"Helping a friend move?" I ask Billy when we're back in the car. "How is Daddy helping a friend move without me knowing about it? And what friend? Is Barry back?"

Billy bats at the set of colorful plastic keys dangling from the car seat handle and doesn't offer any thoughts on the subject as I plug the address on the note into my Garmin GPS. Normally, I wouldn't worry about my husband's whereabouts. But this is New Victor I'm dealing with, and I'm not sure I trust him.

The Garmin directs me to a stone carriage home in a neighborhood a few blocks away from our own house. Victor's blue Ford Taurus is parked in the driveway next to a realtor sign with a banner saying SOLD.

I catch Billy's eyes in the rearview mirror, and we both come to the same conclusion. Just because Daddy isn't at work doesn't mean we can't surprise him with lunch. He'll probably be ready for a break after moving a bunch of furniture and boxes around. I pull in behind the Taurus, pop the liftgate, and pull out the stroller.

I'm just about to shift Billy's carrier over to the stroller when it dawns on me that something isn't right about this picture. No one is unloading any cars or trucks. The front door is closed, and no boxes or plants are stacked around on the front stoop. There's no activity whatsoever. There's just a big, quiet house with my husband's car parked outside.

I take a long, careful look at the house. Thick, light-blocking shades cover all the openings except for a large bay window near the front door. Someone sure likes their privacy. I decide to do a little recon before moving Billy, and stick the stroller back in the car.

I hear music playing as I approach the front door. Grasping the doorknocker, I'm about to strike it against the shiny brass plate when I hear low voices coming from inside: Victor and a woman. I can't make out their words, but the voices sound intimate—like the conversations of old friends—or lovers.

After laying the knocker back down against the door, I step off the stoop, slide into the space between the house and some juniper bushes, and work my way over to the bay window. Two bushy citrus trees full of fruit—maybe kumquats or limes—block my view of the living room's dim interior. Through the leaves, I see Victor and a woman together on the couch. My heart pounds in my chest as I creep along the bottom edge of the window, trying for a better view. I reach a narrow gap between plants where I see Victor's face gazing at the naked young woman writhing on his lap. Now I understand why things have been so strange. New Victor is in love.

As I'm standing there, struggling to breathe and fighting back tears, my shock turns to horror as I watch long, leathery wings unfurl from the woman's back. Her beautiful silhouette morphs into something hard and angular. Instead of being repulsed, Victor's attraction only seems to intensify. My husband pulls the creature down into a long, sensual kiss and turns his head to expose his neck. I see a flash of teeth as the monster begins to feed.

I drop down on my knees in panic, praying they didn't see me. *What is that thing? Am I hallucinating?* My heartbeat resonates through my body like a lone drum beating cadence at an Irish funeral. It's cool and damp under the bay window, and part of me wants to stay here and rest.

But my son needs me. I can't stay here. I use the pounding rhythm in my head to drive myself forward, crawling through the bushes back to the car.

Billy giggles at me when I throw open the car door and jump in behind the wheel. My only thought is to put distance between my son and whatever the hell that thing is. We race home, where I pack some things in the car and prepare to leave.

I place the bag from the diner and Victor's work note on the kitchen counter, adding a note of my own.

Victor,

Billy and I wanted to surprise you today with lunch. Instead, you and that monster surprised us. You need to get away and get some help before that thing kills you. But first, you need to get the hell out of my house.

Don't follow us.

I'm heading to the door when I realize my plan won't work. Running blindly away will let the creature know that I saw it. And Victor knows where my family and friends live. Any place we go will only put the people I love in danger. Billy's eyes signal agreement as he watches me from the business end of his Mickey Mouse formula bottle. I pocket both notes and write a new one to buy some time.

My Personal Space

Hey honey,

Mom and Dad called and asked Billy and me to come visit. You'll have to fend for yourself for a few days. I should be back home by the weekend, but Mom asked if Billy could possibly stay a little longer. That's up to you, but I could sure use the sleep.

Love,

- Rachel

P.S. - Your bologna sandwich is in the fridge.

Grabbing the still-warm bag of diner food off the counter, I hook my arm through the baby carrier handle, step into the garage, and pull the door closed behind me.

* * *

I do a lot of thinking and talking during the four-hour drive to my hometown on the Eastern Shore of Maryland—most of it with tears streaming down my face. "What was that creature? A demon? Alien? Vampire? It looked like something out of one of those old vampire movies--like a female Nosferatu. One minute it was a woman, and the next . . . . And how could my Victor get involved with something like that? Since Billy arrived, Victor has always either been home or at work. He didn't have time for an affair . . . ."

"Listen to me. I'm talking about that monster like it's a real person. Victor isn't having an affair. He's a victim. That demon or vampire or whatever the hell it is tricked him, somehow. Maybe the creature hypnotized him so that it could feed off of him like the vampires in those movies . . . . But if he's hypnotized, how can I get him away from her—from it? I don't think there's a support group for this. Do I call the police? A psychiatrist? A priest?"

Billy hangs on my every word until his belly is full and his bottle is empty. Somewhere around the Bay Bridge, he falls asleep with the bottle dangling out of his mouth, leaving me muttering to myself. After glancing at him through the rearview mirror, I do the rest of my planning in silence.

When we get to town, my first stop is the library, where my love of science began years ago. The familiar scents of books and Murphy's Oil Soap greet me like old friends as I carry my sleeping son through the heavy front door and set his car seat down by the librarian's desk. An elderly lady sits behind the desk, staring through thick spectacles at the computer screen in front of her.

"Hi, Mrs. Price," I say as the woman turns to look my way. Her weathered old face lights up in a happy grin as she runs around the desk and pulls me into a warm hug. "Miss Rachel Wilson," she says. "Aren't you a sight for sore eyes! I haven't seen you in years."

"Rachel Boulanger now," I say, reaching over and touching the car seat handle. "And this is little Billy."

My Personal Space

"It's good to see you, Rachel," says the librarian, bending down to smile at my son. "And a treat to finally meet Master William in person. Your parents come in here at least once a week, and I've seen many a picture of this handsome young lad."

Mrs. Price straightens up and looks back at me. "What can I help you with, Rachel? Are you looking for some summer reading ideas?"

On the drive down, I decided not to tell anyone about Victor. At best, hearing my story might make people think I'm crazy. At worst, it could put them in danger. Instead, I worked out a plausible-sounding lie.

"I wish I was, Mrs. Price, but I have an odd request. I'm taking a writing course while staying home with Billy, and my professor is kind of difficult. Instead of a final exam, he handed each of us a theme based on old folk tales. We need to build a report incorporating the original tale and any relevant facts we find in historical books and newspapers. Most importantly, our report needs to be believable. It has to feel true."

"I decided to come here so that Mom and Dad can hang out with Billy while I work and because I remember how helpful you always were throughout high school and college. I don't know anyone else who delves into their research quite the way that you do."

The old librarian smiles. "Of course, I'll be happy to help, dear. It sounds like fun. And we'll have the entire place to ourselves most days until school lets out. What is this odd theme of yours?"

Relieved, I give my old friend another big hug.

"Thank you, Mrs. Price! My assignment is *How to kill a vampire.*"

Postcards from Earth

* * *

After a quick flurry through the aisles, Mrs. Price sends me home with a stack of books. I was already planning to begin my search with Bram Stoker's *Dracula*, but she adds a few other books to my pile, including *The Queen of the Damned*, by Anne Rice and *Salem's Lot*, by Stephen King. Other books contain old poems by Lord Byron, Samuel Taylor Coleridge, and Johann Wolfgang von Goethe.

From the library, I drive to my parents' house, where I repeat my cover story to Mom and Dad before sitting down for dinner. My parents' old Doberman, Rocky, sits nearby, hoping for any roasted chicken I can spare. Victor calls during dinner, and Mom passes the phone around the table so everyone can talk to him. From the looks on my parents' faces, I can tell that I'm the only one who knows it's New Victor they're speaking with. When my turn comes, I hold the phone next to Billy's ear. "Talk to Daddy!" I say as our son concentrates on picking up a Cheerio. After a few minutes, I end the call and let Billy return to his dinner.

Once Billy is in bed, I begin my research. The stories in the books pull me in, but I resist the urge to relax and read. Instead, I skim each page, entering everything I think might be useful into a spreadsheet on my laptop and filling pages of additional notes in my engineering notebook. I need to save my husband, if he can be saved, and get rid of that monster, if it's possible. I can read later.

I start with the poems. They all tell similar stories about monsters crawling out of graves, hypnotizing their victims, and drinking their blood.

My Personal Space

There isn't much useful in the poems, but I write down that dogs can detect vampires, iron weakens the creatures, and fire kills them.

Next, I dive into the books. *Dracula* contains most of the things I know about vampires. Garlic and communion bread repel the creatures. Vampires leave no shadows, and their reflections don't show up in mirrors. They killed Dracula by driving a wooden stake through his heart and cutting off his head. I read about Renfield, Dracula's half-human servant. *Is Victor like Renfield?* Dracula is super strong and can shapeshift into wolves, bats, and other animals. *The Queen of the Damned* book links vampires back to ancient Egypt and says they die if exposed to sunlight. *Salem's Lot* uses holy water and crosses to fight vampires, but only if the wielder has faith.

I enter all of these "facts" into my laptop and spend the last hour before going to bed organizing my spreadsheet in a way that makes sense.

Tuesday

After morning coffee, I leave Billy in Mom's capable hands and head to the library. Mrs. Price is already there, piling more books on a table next to the front desk. I wasn't aware there were so many vampire books. She even included a stack of old *Dark Shadows* and *Bugs Bunny* VHS tapes. After a morning hug, she points to a nearby table and instructs me to place the books there after reading them. "In case we need to recheck them."

I jump right in, following the same skimming method I used last night. I set aside modern books, thinking the truth must lie further back. I pick up the 1840s *Varney the Vampire* series by James Malcolm Rymer. After that, I read a 1748 poem by Heinrich August Ossenfelder called *The Vampire*, and work my way backward in time, looking for patterns.

I find something interesting. Vampire myths originated in Bulgaria, but they were thought to be malevolent spirits like ghosts or poltergeists. They didn't suck blood or even have bodies. Only after German soldiers invaded Slavic countries in the late 1600s did vampires take the form they have today. Stories of blood-sucking corpses hunting victims at night spread throughout Europe. Catholics believed the vampires were dead bodies controlled by demons, and priests developed elaborate burial rituals to ensure that the dead stayed dead. I go through the remaining books on the table, and a pattern begins to emerge.

- Vampires began appearing wherever crusading Christians invaded other non-Christian societies, like those of the Slavs and Greeks.
- Christian objects, such as crosses, communion bread, and holy water repelled the monsters, as long as the wielders had faith.
- Other objects worked to slow the creatures down, such as garlic, roses, and iron.
- There were ways to detect vampires, using dogs, mirrors, shadows, and candles.
- Vampires were immortal, but died in bright sunlight, from being burned, or by cutting off their heads.
- Driving stakes through vampire's hearts could kill or immobilize them. White Ash, White Oak, and Hawthorn wood worked the best.

My Personal Space

Information about vampire servants and lovers is less clear. In some stories, these thralls, as they were called, withered and died after contact with the vampire. In others, the victim thrived and appeared younger. Some thralls had the same powers and weaknesses as their vampire masters. Others were just human.

But there was no way to cure a vampire's thrall in any of the books. Once someone ingested the blood of a vampire, they were linked to the creature forever. And when a vampire died, their thralls died with them. If those things are true, I might have an unthinkable task ahead of me. I need to find out if my husband is a vampire or thrall. And if he's a vampire, I might have to drive him away or even kill him to protect my family. The thought makes my chest feel tight and my stomach lurch.

I put that gruesome possibility aside for now and take long, slow breaths until my panic is under control. Kidlin's Law says, "If you write a problem down clearly, then the problem is half solved." I need to develop a test to determine if my husband is one of those things. A test that won't harm Victor or tip him off that I had witnessed his strange affair.

I'll bring my parents' dog when I return home. Rocky always loved Victor. If he still does, Victor is probably okay. I'll watch for other things, too, like shadows and reflections in mirrors. It's not much of a plan, but it's something. I sketch out a quick flowchart of the test in my notebook.

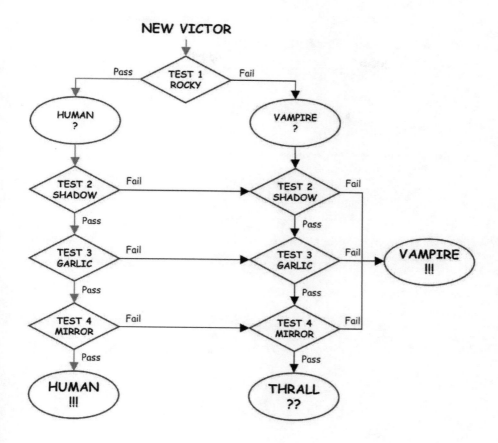

"What if you're wrong?" asks Mrs. Price over my shoulder.

"What?" I ask.

"What's if you're wrong about something controlling your husband?"

"I don't know what you mean. I'm… um… I'm writing a paper on how to kill a vampire—"

My Personal Space

"I can't pretend to understand what you're going through, lass. I really can't," says Mrs. Price. "But I've been a librarian for over thirty years and was a school teacher before that. I know what writing a paper looks like, and this isn't it."

My old friend smiles. "You're not researching how one might kill a vampire," she says. "You're trying to find out if your husband is one."

The old librarian eases herself down into the chair beside mine and grasps both of my hands. "But, dear, before you go and do something that might cause harm or wreck your marriage, consider seeing a counselor and talking over what's making you feel this way. Postpartum depression anxiety is a real thing, and it can take a lot of strange forms.

I'm on the verge of telling Mrs. Price what I saw at that house when she slips a book about postpartum depression into my home reading pile. I decide to keep silent.

She turns and points to my flowchart, once again acting as my vampire researcher.

"And I don't know if I would put much stock in any of these tests, dear. Vampires not having shadows or reflections might be something Bram Stoker made up. Those things weren't in the earlier stories and poems we read."

She tapped my flowchart a few times. "But keep the mirror test in. Priests still use mirrors to try and detect demonic possession."

* * *

That evening, I lie back in bed with Billy curled up next to me and read stories until he drifts off to sleep. I don't feel like I'm experiencing postpartum depression or any other type of anxiety other than the natural fear that comes from watching a winged vampire creature slurp blood out of my husband's neck. I consider telling my parents what's happening, but again, I stay silent. Instead, I decide to return home tomorrow, run my test, and go from there.

Wednesday

After morning coffee with Mom and Dad, I pepper Billy's face with a week's worth of kisses and head out to the car. I open the car door for Rocky, who climbs into the back seat and sticks his head out the window. Rocky loves road trips.

On the way out of town, I run by the hardware store for a box of long iron nails and several strips of white oak. As I head to the checkout line, I spot an intimidating-looking lumber maul with a sharp blade and place that in my cart. Next, I drive by our old church and fill several baby food jars with Christening water. My last stop is Grandmom's old family property, where I cut bunches of wild pink and white Carolina roses off of the fence line, thorns and all. If I'm heading to Crazytown, I might as well bring along a vampire kit.

On the way back to Virginia, I run through various scenarios in my head. I think about each test and the best way to execute them without Victor knowing what I'm up to. Vampires were strong, fast, and quick to anger in all the books I read. If I decide to act, I've got to take him by surprise, or else I'll fail.

When we get back home, I spend the afternoon completing my kit. I dig my grandmother's old crucifix pendant and a silver hand mirror out of a dresser drawer. I place rose bouquets all over the house where Victor can't avoid their sweet fragrance. I go to the grocery store and pick up Victor's favorite spaghetti ingredients, including a mesh bag full of fresh garlic bulbs. The house soon overflows with delicious but powerful aromas that Victor used to love. Afterward, Rocky and I sit on the back steps sawing, sharpening, and chewing on a dozen wooden stakes I hope I'll never use. I put the crucifix around my neck, place the vampire kit items in a white canvas beach bag, and stash the bag and lumber maul in the pantry. Van Helsing would be proud.

* * *

I'm dumping a box of spaghetti noodles into a pot of boiling water when Rocky springs up from the kitchen rug. His chest rumbles like thunder as he races to the front door. He paces back and forth, yowling and whining in a way I never heard him do before… like he's afraid.

I turn the water down to a low simmer and glance out the front window. The Taurus is pulling into the driveway. New Victor is home. Rocky bounds past me to the kitchen when the garage door rumbles open. Growling deep in his chest, the big Doberman scratches and bites at the door to the garage. His hackles stand on edge from the base of his muscular neck down to his stumpy tail. My chest tightens, and I struggle to breathe. I'm not ready for this, and I fight the urge to lock the door and call the police.

"Rachel! Are you alright in there?" calls Victor from the other side of the door. "Is that Rocky? Can I come in?"

When he hears Victor's voice, Rocky snorts and barks, keeping his body between me and the door. *He's trying to keep Victor away from me,* I think. *Good dog.*

But I need to know. I need to run my tests. "Hold on," I say. "Let me put the dog outside."

Rocky whines and moans as I grasp his collar and lead him onto the back porch. I slip back inside and shut the door. The big dog jumps up and places both paws on the door's window frame, continuing to bark and growl. I walk to the pantry, reach into my vampire kit, twist the lid off one of the Christening water jars, and set it on a shelf.

"Okay!" I say. "You can come in. Rocky is outside."

When Victor enters the kitchen, Rocky digs at the doorframe, growling and baring his teeth. He's never acted this way before, and in my head, I think **TEST 1** *is a* **FAIL**. I check for shadows on the kitchen floor but don't see any from either Victor *or* me. I guess there are too many lights in here, and I forgot to check earlier. Chalk **TEST 2** up to Murphy's Law, for now. *Anything that can go wrong, will.*

"What's the matter with Rocky?" asks Victor, looking puzzled. "He used to love me."

My Personal Space

The big dog stomps against the door with both paws when Victor speaks.

Victor sniffs, frowning. "And what's that smell, Rachel? Did something spill? The whole kitchen smells like rotten garlic!"

"I'm making spaghetti just the way you like it, babe," I say, trying to sound normal. "I used fresh garlic this time. Maybe that's why it smells stronger. I was planning to use it on the garlic bread, too—".

"Maybe just make toast," says Victor. "I think that garlic must be bad. It smells disgusting!" **TEST 3** *is also a* **FAIL**. *I'm starting to get scared.*

"I can't smell it, but okay, toast it is. And I'll see if I can fix the sauce."

I move into the pantry and pretend to sort through cans and boxes for ingredients. I reach into my vampire kit, pull out the silver hand mirror, and slowly raise it above my shoulder to peer back at Victor. His reflection is visible, but his hair appears long and patchy in the mirror, and his face and arms look infected and covered with pustules. A tangle of web-like strands, the color of dried blood, float all around him through the air like a thin, puffy cocoon. The red strands writhe and pulse as if they're alive, sometimes touching down on Victor's flesh and digging through his body like worms.

I'm lowering the mirror back into my bag when Victor's hand is suddenly gripping my arm. I've never seen anyone move so fast. His other hand caresses my shoulder as he reaches over to pull the mirror out of my hand.

"And this is the wretched thing that has done the mischief," he says from behind me. "A foul bauble of man's vanity."

That quote was in the *Dracula* book. *Victor knows what I'm doing.*

Victor smirks and releases my arm. He walks to the garbage can and tosses the mirror inside. "Away with it!"

I pull the Christening water off the shelf while he's looking the other way. As he turns back around, I splash it into his face. "Get away from me!" I yell. "You're not my husband!"

Victor smiles grimly, shaking his head. "Rachel, honey, it doesn't work that way," he says.

My throat tightens, and I pull Grandmom's crucifix out of my shirt, backing away from him. "G-g-get out of my house!" I stutter, trying to be brave.

There's a crash as Rocky throws himself against the door.

Victor pulls a few paper towels from the roll on the counter and wipes his face, stepping toward me. "And neither does your fancy jewelry," he says, still smiling.

I take another step backward and butt up against the stove. I feel hot steam rising from the pot and hear the roiling water behind me. "Why are you here?" I ask. "What do you want from me?"

Rocky's barking is louder.

My Personal Space

"I just want you to love me, Rachel," Victor says. "I want things to go back the way they were before—" He turns as if staring at some imaginary object off in the distance. "Before you saw us that day—"

I twist and grab both handles on the pot of boiling spaghetti. I turn around to throw when Victor's hands are suddenly on top of mine, holding them firmly in place. He takes the pot gently from my grip, sets it back on the stove, and shuts off the heat. *Game over.*

"And you want that too," he says. "I know you do. I can feel it."

I do want that. But I don't think it can ever be that way again. I move to step past him, away from the stove. Victor slaps me hard across the face and shoves me back against the stove. I taste blood in my mouth.

Rocky barks from the other side of the door.

Victor grabs my shoulders, forcing me to face him. His eyes swirl and sparkle, drawing me in. The room fades away, and his face is all I see.

"We will have it again, Rachel," he says soothingly. "We'll have it all."

Victor's pupils melt away into two fiery tunnels, pulling me closer. He licks his lips as my body leans toward him as if I'm on the verge of falling. I hear soft crackling and tearing sounds from the dark strands writhing around us, and I sense the cocoon opening as it spreads apart to envelop me within.

Victor pulls my crucifix over my head and tosses it onto the counter. I'm helpless to do anything as he tilts my neck to one side.

Postcards from Earth

I'm sorry, Billy.... Forgive me for my failure.

There's a loud crash of breaking glass, and something dark flies through the air and slams into Victor. Rocky. My vision clears as the two spin away across the kitchen floor. I shake off my fog, rush to the pantry, and grab the lumber maul. Victor's lips pull back, exposing razor-sharp fangs. He howls like a wild animal. I can see his dying, infected flesh and the raw madness in his eyes. The strange, dark threads buzz angrily around the room in an expanding cloud.

Victor regains his footing, grabs Rocky, and slams the dog down onto the kitchen table, splintering wood and bones. Rocky howls out in pain, and blood oozes from his mouth and nose. Victor growls and leans in for the kill.

I swing the heavy maul with all my strength, and it slams down onto Victor's neck just above his shoulders. He falls forward, screaming as dark blood spurts from the gash. Rocky yelps as Victor drops on top of him.

I lift the axe again and thrust it back down, aiming for the same spot on Victor's neck. My aim is true, and his blood begins to flow out in a thick stream. His body collapses forward, and he stops moving. "Wait, Rachel," he moans.

I swing again. I miss my target this time, and the maul slams into Victor's shoulder. Rocky cries out from the impact.

"Stop, Rachel. You're hurting Rocky," whispers Victor.

My Personal Space

Victor looks like he's helpless to move, so I roll him over onto the floor and look over my dog's broken body. Rocky's front leg appears shattered, and several ribs poke out from his chest at odd angles. Shards of glass protrude from his legs and torso from where he jumped through the window. There's a lot of blood, and I worry that a rib may have pierced his lungs. Grabbing a dish towel, I wipe the blood away from his nose and mouth. Rocky licks my hand weakly as if apologizing for not coming sooner. He growls, and his eyes dart toward Victor.

Steely fingers grab my arm. I look over and see the dark, swirling threads spinning frantically around the gash on Victor's neck—and watch him healing right in front of my eyes. Arteries and veins rise from the wound and twist themselves together. The blood pooling on the floor around him begins seeping back into his body.

I roll away, pulling myself free of his grip.

"Wait, Rachel," says Victor, his voice sounding stronger. "Help me."

His eyes begin to sparkle and swirl.

I swing the maul again and again until the blade cuts through muscle and bones. The dark strands begin swirling faster, repairing the damage almost as fast as I can inflict it. I panic and continue to chop.

"Nooo," moans Victor as I hack away like a madman. Dark blood and bits of flesh and bone splatter across the floor and walls of the kitchen. I don't stop swinging until the skin of Victor's neck peels back, and the ceramic floor tile shatters beneath my blade. Decapitation isn't enough to stop him, and I watch as the strange threads reach outward and weave through the pieces of his body, pulling them together and connecting them. I scream and rush forward, kicking Victor's head across the room. The bloody webbing stretches and finally snaps, and the head tumbles a few feet away, facing the wall. Dark threads swirl and buzz around Victor's head, but the webbing strands around his neck and body become sluggish and fade.

"You're killing me, Rachel," whispers Victor's head from its place on the floor. "Help me. Bring me back over to my body. Please—"

I ignore the creature who used to be my husband. Instead, I soothe my dog as I think about what to do next. I need to get Rocky to the vet, but I need to do some cleaning first. I grab Victor's head by the hair, toss it into a garbage bag, and throw it into the big chest freezer in the garage. The dark, writhing strands follow along, buzzing like flies on a carcass as I lower the lid and twist the latch closed. "Noooo," moans the head from inside the box. Its voice is muffled and low.

When I get back to the kitchen, my situation hits me. Now that the monster has been defeated, my house is just another murder scene, and I'm the one left holding the lumber maul. According to Gilbert's Law, *"The biggest problem with a job is that no one tells you what to do."* I'll have to figure this out all by myself. I wrap Victor's body in an old painter's tarp and tape the seams with duct tape. I give the kitchen a cursory wipe-down and pull the curtains over the broken back window.

After gently laying Rocky on top of some old blankets in the back of the Jeep, I clean the blood and glass out of his fur with tweezers and a dishtowel and drive him to the animal hospital. The veterinarian there doesn't question me when I say that Rocky got hit by a car. Once he is stable and resting, I head back home.

I stop at Hechinger's to buy cleaning supplies and make an appointment to get my door window repaired. The next several days are bloody and disgusting as I hack Victor's body into small pieces, put the pieces into plastic bags, and drop them into dumpsters and garbage cans all over the county. At the end of each day, I drive to the animal hospital and spend an hour or two comforting Rocky, bringing him treats, and telling him I'll take him home soon.

I don't touch Victor's head or heart, which are both wrapped in strands of that strange, swirling webbing material. My house feels like some haunted freak show. Whenever I approach the freezer, the head calls out to me. The heart still beats on a shelf in my refrigerator. I place both out in the sun one day when no one else is around, but nothing happens. Apparently, sunlight doesn't kill them. Victor begins to whisper, "Help me, Ani!" and I throw the head back into the freezer.

Last Days

I slide my mountain bike into Victor's car and drive to West Virginia to find the remote road where Barry disappeared. I wipe the car down a final time, and roll it over an embankment. After several hours of pedaling, I make it back home and get some rest.

The following day, after a deep and dreamless sleep, I go to the kitchen and start the coffee maker. Today, I'm going to pick up Rocky from the hospital and drive to my parents' house. When I get there, I plan to take my father's boat out and use chains and concrete blocks to sink Victor's head into a deep part of the Chesapeake Bay where he used to like to fish.

I pull our old Coleman cooler off a shelf in the garage and lower my husband's head inside. "Help me, Ani," it whispers. I carry the cooler into the kitchen and set it on Victor's chair. I explain to Victor that I will stay vigilant for the rest of my life in case that vampire, Ani, ever returns. I say that I'm going to tell the truth to our son and that I'm going to teach Billy how to kill vampires. Sighing, I finally hit play on the CD player, listen to the Cranberries, sip my coffee, and sit with my husband one last time.

I'm about to leave when I get an idea. I place the heart into a Tupperware bowl, writhing strands and all. I stick the container in the microwave oven and hit start. After a few minutes, the webbing fades away, and the heart stops beating. Afterward, when I open the cooler, the head is silent, and the threads are all gone.

How do you kill a vampire? Simple. Microwave its heart.

My Personal Space

Acknowledgements

Thank you to my family and friends for their constant support and encouragement.

Thank you to my "Brain Trust" Ben and Sam who let me bounce my crazy ideas off of them.

Thank you to the Writers of Chantilly for welcoming me into their group, reviewing my stories, and taking the time to try and help me become a better writer.

Thank you to my editor Christine Cartwright for her patience and advice.

And thank you to all of the folks who took time out of their busy schedules to jump into one of my stories and try to help save the world.

Acknowledgements

Postcards from Earth

About the Author

TOM STERLING was born in the small town of Crisfield on Maryland's Eastern Shore. A place where stories and songs float out on the wind like the salty aroma of fresh marsh grasses.

He moved to Northern Virginia, where he worked as an engineer in the defense industry for forty years. While there, stories continued floating out to him, but they came from dusty engineering notebooks and long-forgotten Cold War circuitry.

These days, Tom spends his time remembering all the old stories and writing them down.

Tom writes a collection of short science fiction and fantasy stories describing ordinary people thrown into extraordinary situations. The series is called *Postcards from Earth* and can be found on Amazon. His stories and poems have been published in numerous anthologies, and two of his poems were featured on National Public Radio.

He lives in Virginia with his wife, MyPhuong.

www.tomsterling.com

Made in the USA
Middletown, DE
16 October 2024